K.N.I.F.E.P.O.I.N.T
The First Mission.
A Sojourn Of Lies Island Iced Tea

Mitrajit Biswas

Ukiyoto Publishing

All global publishing rights are held by

Ukiyoto Publishing

Published in 2023

Content Copyright © Mitrajit Biswas

ISBN 9789360497354

All rights reserved.
No part of this publication may be reproduced, transmitted, or stored in a retrieval system, in any form by any means, electronic, mechanical, photocopying, recording or otherwise, without the prior permission of the publisher.

The moral rights of the author have been asserted.

This is a work of fiction. Names, characters, businesses, places, events, locales, and incidents are either the products of the author's imagination or used in a fictitious manner. Any resemblance to actual persons, living or dead, or actual events is purely coincidental.

This book is sold subject to the condition that it shall not by way of trade or otherwise, be lent, resold, hired out or otherwise circulated, without the publisher's prior consent, in any form of binding or cover other than that in which it is published.

www.ukiyoto.com

Contents

The New Era Beckons	1
The Coded Puzzle Of The Bigger Picture	5
64 Squares Of Black And White Pieces	9
All Lines Are Not Straight	13
The Mirror Behind The Mirror	17
Seeking The Truth Leads To A Bunch Of Lies	20
Operation Golden Crescent Triangle	24

The New Era Beckons

It had been around 3 years since I last visited Istanbul. Around 2016 I had visited this beautiful city for a security meeting. India was participating in a N.A.T.O. (North Atlantic Treaty Organization) security summit as special invitee and I had just joined "Knowledge gathering unit for National Intelligence and Forensic Expertise for Prevention of Organized Internal and National Threats" with a fancied acronym K.N.I.F.E.P.O.I.N.T. on a deputation from Intelligence Bureau. This was a new unit created as a multi-agency and cutting-edge intelligence gathering mechanism to coordinate with agencies such as NIA, I.B, R&AW and military as well as economic intelligence unit. I was put on Central Asia desk. Those were my early taking on the challenge to protect India's interests as the world was now on the brink of a new threshold.

Coming from a small hilly town of the north of Bengal and managing to come up here was a part of the story that may sound cliched. I got a decent education thanks to the support of my parents. The journey from the hamlet of North Bengal to the security meeting in Istanbul had been quite a journey. However, my life started to take a turn from there. I was supposed to attend the meet but there was something else I was sent for. I was sent to uncover a deep covert operation unit in Istanbul operating with plans to push drugs, separatism and other issues that was coming in greater measures. I was assigned a local support named Umut one of our close associates in Turkey to get started. I was excited to contact our local asset. I was asked to shadow a high-profile Pakistani target which I will disclose later as the story unfolds.

The asset I was looking to shadow was an asset who had made inroads in Kashmir radical elements. Preliminary intelligence suggests that she was leading a network to honeytrap several Kashmiri youths. Only some years later it was found out that this asset had managed to infiltrate up to the level of DGP. I was assigned to shadow Ruksana who was the cultural attaché in Pakistan consulate at Istanbul. Umut was a part of the Turkish counter terrorism unit who had been working on some inputs with our intelligence agency before.

I was staying at a hotel close to the meeting centre at the convention which was on this side of the Bosporus. It was the month of May, and I was supposed to stay in Istanbul for around three days. After the meeting we were supposed to go on a city tour. I knew that this was the time to look out for any other delegates especially the one I was here for. There were some members of the Pakistan delegates staying near my hotel. However, till then my only way was to attach a standard GPS nano chip in the brief case of one of the delegates. The range was good however I needed a personal asset to help me track the cultural attaché. My desk boss had told me to contact Umut as he would give me precisely the time and place to meet.

The call came from Umut on my local cell phone as he gave me the location of a Turkish coffee shop. He said he would be sitting on the third chair in the left-hand side of the café. I reached the café and saw him in a black jacket. He was a sharp looking guy with a light beard. He was now working for a private security firm. He had been working with the Indian government since the Arab crisis to tip off on I.S.I.S. (Islamic State of Iraq & Syria officially known as Daeesh) expansion and recruitment plans apart from Pakistani and Chinese influenced movements in the gulf. Tip offs used to come from him on various important events in west Asia.

He was of great help with his inputs as I was informed by my desk boss that he had strong contacts for information sharing on supplies of army, money and drug trafficking routes and networks. Umut started to speak as he said that he had been providing inputs to the Indian government since the emergence of ISIS. He was actively trying to provide information on the pockets of the Pakistan infiltration agents working in Syria, Iraq, Lebanon, Libya and pockets of Jordan as well as Turkey. Now the talks shifted to the present times where there was immense possibility of a cell working within Turkey and Azerbaijan area being backed by someone high profile from the Pakistan consulate.

Umut told me that I needed to keep a close eye on Ruksana who was here as a cultural attaché. She is generally seen frequenting the border areas of Turkey close to Azerbaijan. I told him bluntly that I needed more information than some superficial information. He said that later tonight he would give me more details as he left behind a card of Doner shop and signalled 10 p.m. before he left the café.

I came back to my hotel room, and I was wondering that how could this play out in the broader scheme of things. It all seemed like there were so many chess pieces on a chess board. We already had so much of problems back at home, now what more was this cultural attached named Ruksana Nazir cooking up. It was all a matter of connecting the dots. There had been issues already in the India-China conflict in the Himalayas and the new security challenges emerging for India. It was time for me to go back to the grand bazar as it was around 10 p.m. as I reached around 10:05 p.m. Umut was there as he had a smirk on face although I did admire his punctuality. He looked at me and said that I must be very eager to find out the real information as I had asked him for. Then he started that the rea place of interest for me would be Azerbaijan-Turkey border. After that he took out an envelope from his belt. The envelop was heavy and I was eager to find out what was inside it.

The envelope had a bunch of photographs as I could see in one of the pictures the location was near the Turkish border. She was seen in the photograph handing something to a likely Chinese diplomat. Along with the pictures the names were also mentioned of the ones in the pictures. The names also included details of the designation and the picture I saw mentioned the man as one of the trade delegates. Umut looked at me and said don't be surprised as his local assets had taken those pictures. It was during the Turkish international trade fair and most likely the talks were on funding students from Pakistan to study in Turkey. Umut said below these photographs I would find an Indian named Jayesh Singh who runs a local spices store in the grand bazar area itself.

Apparently, he was the owner of a small grocery stores in Istanbul, Ankara, Gaziantep and one near the Turkey-Azerbaijan border. He was the local asset who was the main courier for Ruksana. He was the one who used to overlook into the flow of money being moved into Europe for setting up local community centres across the mosques in Europe. The routes were being used one through Germany and France and the one through West Asia into Turkey. The money trail most likely originated from China which was being funnelled through Pakistan. All these information was there in the two pages encoded in Morse code. All I could understand was that Ruksana was present infiltrating mosques in Europe and the recruitment of students in Turkey who were coming in from Pakistan. However, the real conundrum lied in the joining of connection between the Chinese money, the Pakistani involvement and the possible hatching of nefarious plans from Turkey. To know about all this the key person would be Jayesh Singh and the route between Turkey-Azerbaijan border.

The next day summit went on as usual. My mind had to moved far away from discussion on war games and was solely focused on returning to New Delhi. I asked Umut to keep an eye for Ruksana. However, there were gaps which needed to relate to the dots. I met Umut again before I flew away back to New Delhi. I tried to initiate conversation with Ruksana at the gala dinner, but she was in the company of Turkish and the Chinese delegates. I could not observe much fearing to draw attention. The next day I flew back to Delhi with Umut as my only local source of contact back in Turkey.

The Coded Puzzle Of The Bigger Picture

The discussion at the briefing room went on with the information collected from our local asset. We were created as a deep covert Home Ministry approved multi-agency liaison unit. The unit reported only to the Prime Minister's office and Home Ministry. My immediate boss was Ranjini Sagar who was a dynamic and strong boos and servant of the nation. She had come up from the ranks of military intelligence and had also spent some time in the cipher department.

Our main topic of discussion was based on the problems that may happen in the northern part of India. Especially the scenario with the Chinese was our main concern. The main discussion was on the reports and the materials provided by Umut which pointed at the weapons, money and human resources happening through the nexus of China and Pakistan. Also, the flow of Drugs and the money which was happening through narcotics smuggling was being used to buy out higher ranked officers as well as honey trapping them.

We devised a strategy to set up surveillance units as 40 names based on their importance in the Indian defence establishment, location and accessibility were kept in the list. The names were mostly from Jammu, Kashmir, Rajasthan, Punjab, Uttarakhand and Uttar Pradesh. However, our cyber team had to constantly monitor and lookout for the Chinese or Pakistan based trail of any kind from even an individual in the list. The Chinese had been creating problems in the chicken's neck and Doklam area as well as Arunachal.

The attacks on Uri as well as the attacks on Northeast India with certain trickle routes through Bangladesh and Myanmar and the names of Ruksana as well as Jayesh can all be connected. Now the main onus of the teams which were being put on surveillance duty was to monitor and track the people on the list. Whereas the rest of the team were to be involved in deciphering the pictures and the two pages note which accompanies the pictures needed to be seen for possible clues and forensic scrutiny.

Two weeks had passed by then as after that one a Thursday I got an update from Umut. He called me up as I was about to go off to sleep as Turkey was just behind our time. He told me to go on the secure line which I did as he said that a top level IB operative in Jammu was probably involved in sending information to the I.S.I. (Inter Services Intelligence). He said that he would send in more details. I probed him to tell me that how he got the information. He told me that he had activated his local assets who had managed to get access to calls originating from his shop. Most of them were internet calls but the calls were directed t Jammu. Also, his local assets had tracked a man a week back who came here on a different name but was most likely I.B. (Intelligence Bureau) operative. The name once he confirms he will send over more information.

His computer was accessed by breaking into his shop where the money trail was going to third party accounts. The difficult aspect was to pinpoint the person and what was his connection to the Indian establishment. The shop being broken into probably may have alerted Jayesh, but Umut said as the local asset for Indian agencies he needed to get more information. He said that a person of higher rank was flying to Dubai quite frequently and someone else who was there in Uttar Pradesh IAS ranks who had recently purchased a huge property in Mumbai. The names needed to be confirmed now. The person probably visited Nepal and Bhutan a few times as the computer records of Jayesh had quite a few hotel booking reservations of Patan and Paro.

The idea was now to get into the details of tracking the people who were using the servers to withdraw or transfer money. The N.T.R.O. or National Technical Research Organization came to our rescue. The names and the identities had been confirmed of the high-profile targets who were cross checked based on surveillance records. The number of transactions and the volume of the money transacted were the first genuine proofs that indeed there was information trading going on.

My desk chief Ranjini told me to set up a physical surveillance team of the targeted individuals. The main task was connecting the dots between the confirmed inside targets and how they were involved. The blueprint was there however the main task was to see the bigger picture assuming that our targeted profiles were also being careful. We had to keep a constant watch on them. However, things did not turn out as easy as we thought it would. Two of our trails went cold which came to haunt us later. The I.B. officer and the IAS whom we were after became suddenly untraceable.

The information sources about them had dried up although local sources informed that one of them had travelled to Bhutan and the other one to Sri Lanka. Apparently, both had gone on a family holiday. Ruksana had not travelled there personally surely but ISI operatives were there. Now the question was what kind of information was being traded. Our surveillance team was on the way to scout for local information sources from Bhutan and Sri Lanka.

Although our local sources confirmed that one the target who was the IB operative Ayan Patel was on his way to Bhutan through North Bengal. My task was to track him till he reached there. I knew the task of tracking him would not be that difficult however eluding the ISI was the part that I needed to look for. After three days our team posted in the border region of Bhutan-West Bengal border confirmed that a forged id card most likely resembling Ayan Patel in the name of Trilok Pandit had crossed the border. It was on the same day that reports of infiltration from Kashmir was emerging.

He was using the road route as I took the same route minutes after I received reports of him crossing the border. My desk boss was also tracking details of Sukhbir Bisht who were looking into his every moment through local agent. The local agents were looking into his movement, and I recalled that there could be far more ISI local operatives in Uttar Pradesh who were crossing the Bangladesh border. The leads that had gone cold probably had smuggled themselves and information through the eastern part of India over to Bangladesh based pro Pakistan organizations.

The other two assets which had gone cold had suddenly emerged as a tip off was received by our desk boss Ranjini. The tip off came from the N.T.R.O. cyber team who had reported that a huge amount of money was transferred from Turkey as the origin sourced that was routed through Switzerland to an account in an offshore account likely in Panama. Although the account number was the same to which frequent transactions were made for last one year. However, the confirmation came because that account number of that bank account was accessed from Durgapur in Bengal and Mathura in Uttar Pradesh.

Two days later following their movement they had moved into Nepal and Bangladesh strictly under our watch. They met with some local associates there as my unit reported that probably they were involved with local madrasa. Whereas in Nepal the reports came that our fourth asset was meeting some communist members. They were looking to leave tonight as our local assets in the border region were told to be active. However, we could not wait further as we had confirmed their links to foreign elements. Our assets who worked in border areas as covert unit was told to pick them up just when they crossed into Indian territory.

64 Squares Of Black And White Pieces

The rule to get hold of any spy network was to get hold of the all the pieces. This is why the covert counter insurgency assault unit S.N.I.P.E.R. (Strategic National Intelligence Personnel for Evaluative Response) were activated. They had left the motel, and they were carrying their gear. As planned once they cross the border the agents would take them down apart from snatching their bags which they were carrying as they left their motel.

As planned within a span of four days the four assets were taken into custody. The two from the border areas of Bangladesh and Nepal and the other two from Mathura and Durgapur. The had been taken into custody and from the initial investigation's maps of India, location of space agencies and defence manufacturing plants and two USB sticks. They were kept in black sites locations across four different parts of the country.

I was heading one of the interrogation teams and the maps were carefully studied. Also, the bank details were now checked which showed that there were plans for four of them to meet in Dubai next month. Flight ticket details were recovered from their mobile phones which did not take much time to be decrypted.

Umut called me in the middle of investigation as he asked me to come down to Turkey. He said that he had got some inputs. The inputs were big and therefore he wanted me to personal tell me face to face. I decided to come down to Turkey as it all seemed to come down to where it all started. The same place where I visited Umut last time is where I was waiting this time as well.

Umut came down as usual as he pushed forth a list of names this time in a written piece of paper. He added along with those names that a splinter group of ISIS was formed in Kerala and Lakshadweep who were looking to move to Kashmir and Punjab. The group was named Fateh Hind. The group was apparently recruiting people and funding them from Italy to Turkey. Providing funds for student visa and living costs were being funnelled from this organization via offshore accounts and Pakistan consulate in Turkey.

We had got a very vague idea that what was being planned as sleeper cells and terrorist funding was not something new. Our intelligence teams suggested that there may be a series of low-level attacks which were being planned and then may be a major incident. From the investigation two more names have come up who were active in Gurgaon and Noida. One of them was named Paresh Tomar and the other one is named Rakesh Gill. Apparently, they were the ones who were working as hawala and funding local sleeper cells in Kerala through money transfer agent Syed Muzammil who in turn were helped by Shiba Mondol and Lokesh Raut from Hyderabad for changing account numbers.

Umut told me one more interesting thing that there were certain people who were lobbying in US congress likely from Pakistan and even Turkey to push for more funds into these countries from N.A.T.O. funding. The funnelling of money for grey operational areas is a likely possibility. Most importantly there was another area which was being investigated which is to smuggle N.A.T.O. funded weapons through merchant shipping containers from Turkey to Pakistan and then via Afghan border area into India. It was not only being done for creating tensions in India but in entire South Asia.

Umut told that by tomorrow he would be able to get some information from a housecleaning staff who used to work in Pakistan Consulate and a NATO funded private military firm from UK working in Afghanistan. The person can be useful as he had a lot of contacts which was established during his tenure in Afghanistan during which he had met quite a few Pakistani officers and ground rangers. Umut said however for the meeting to go ahead I should arrange for 10000 USD with 7000 for the guy and 3000 his brokerage fees by tonight over his usual monthly commission. I told him that let me try but, in the meantime, I was wondering something.

There was a team who were there with me and I had passed my audio recording of the meeting for a background check. However, the money was arranged as the next day meeting with the Pakistani house cleaning staff went ahead. A young man with rimless glasses unlike a house cleaning staff looks named Farid met me in a local coffee shop. However, when I met him, he asked for one more thing that he can help me to get more contact and more information if I can arrange a medical visa and sponsored medical treatment in India. He seemed firm as I looked at his eyes.

I told him that I needed at least some preliminary information which he decided to share. He told me that Pakistan had been using their movie stars and even people from around India in the form of aspiring models, two or three producers who were being funded for channelling money into fuelling any matter of socio-economic importance in India via social media. Also using fake videos and provocative news against Muslims in India as well as creating dedicated social media teams to fuel violent debates on social media and then riots was all part of the plan.

He also mentioned at least modelling agency names whose models were being used to lure influential people and connected people with defence establishment in a typical honey trap style. A new model of fish net hooking was used which moves the money through various countries and targeting different high-profile people for tested and valued information which was then passed through sleeper cell networks.

Targeting investments of India which were happening in abroad as well as India was also being done through Chinese help. Using the help of local Pakistani businessmen in middle east there was a steady flow of money happening inro areas of Uttar Pradesh, Bihar and Kerala for fuelling anti India activities.

He said that he can provide more information provided I investigate his demands. I told him that I would certainly investigate his demands. After having Turkish delights and strong Turkish coffee I told them that I would arrange for a meeting very doon. I returned to my hotel around 10 p.m. I was supposed to another guy who was a personal contact of Umut and can trade more information. In the meantime, had called up my desk chief asking for compliance of the request made by Farid.

She said she needed some information as she needed time to check his background information and verify it. Amidst all of this I was wondering about what Farid had said and how could it all connect with the four assets already in our custody. The movement of them across Bangladesh, Nepal apart from the list of names and potential targets received from them and what Rana had said may have connection towards a bigger plan. The names of Fateh Hind and a Riyasat foundation from Uttar Pradesh was floating around. The foundation was funding students in Turkey from various countries.

All Lines Are Not Straight

I was back at my hotel around 10 p.m. when I received a call from Umut. He told me to come down in half an hour at a seaside café. Umut told me his local contact would be a great asset and information source. The guy was a Turkish special force operative in Syria to fight against ISIS and runs a private security consulting firm. I decided to meet him and that's why went ahead with the meeting. The guy was in a leather jacket and short stout man. In the initial 10 minutes he told me about the routes of Afghanistan to Pakistan for getting into India and how I.S.I. (Inter Services Intelligence) agents were getting I.S.I.S (Islamic State of Iraq & Syria officially known as Daeesh) recruits to get into India through funding from the government and local mafia.

He however mentioned that Chabahar port where India was putting in money was now being used by I.S.I. to influence the local authorities there. Narco trafficking and weapons was being done through the port and being smuggled into ports in India for money transfer and weapons smuggling apart from some information trading as well as keeping the local sleeper cells active. The students recruited from Turkey who were of Pakistani, and some Indian origin were local carriers. There were chances of an attack both offline and in the cyber space.

However, the attacks may not happen at strategic places in India but may be adjoining countries. I asked Ruslan whether he can arrange for more specific information and would be duly compensated. Our agency sources also had picked up some information whose transcripts suggested what Ruslan had been saying. Narcotics Control Bureau and N.T.R.O. were also on alert but the difficulty was to connect the drug money trail with cyber terrorism as it is difficult to track operations in the dark web.

Ruslan said that can send a list of maps and shipping companies being used but he would need an account transfer of the money asked by Umut along with his commission. I told him I would fly out tomorrow but before the reply to his offer would be provided.

I called up my boss and told her of the present scenario. It was the second time after Rana that I was asking her for money as she asked if I was confident about his information. She told me that she would let me know by tomorrow morning. I was tired as I went off to sleep. I received the call from Ranjini next morning and she asked for the account number to transfer the money. However, she asked for more specific route details of ships and their company details. Also, can he provide more details on the profile of students being recruited in Turkey.

I reassured to my desk chief that I would try to get the information. I called up Umut and asked for Ruslan and told him that the money had been arranged. I told him that if I can get more information, I can provide him more than the amount he has asked for. I told him that I needed more specific information and wanted to meet him at 3 p.m. as I would leave later in the evening.

I went to a café spot right across the Pakistan embassy as I waited there for around two hours to catch a glimpse of Ruksana. I had been informed by our local agents that all embassies in the vicinity generally used to close by 9 p.m. but on certain days the Pakistan embassy used to close by 11 p.m. Around two or three people on certain days used to stay back. This could be all routine affair although I did not catch a glimpse of Ruksana. My time to meet Ruslan had come up as I was given a location on the outskirts of Istanbul. It was his country house and he asked me to meet there.

As soon as I reached the location suddenly two individuals sprang up and kicked me to the grass area near the entrance of the house. Ruslan peaked out of the window as indeed they were hired guns and likely local assets of our friendly neighbour. Ruslan was about to shoot from his second floor as it was not needed as they fired two shots which missed before they were pulled in by a grey SUV. Ruslan rushed towards the entrance as I went inside. He gave me a glass of scotch as I gulped it in.

Ruslan sad that if I was fine as I replied I was all good and told him that if he gave more information, I could provide him more money than he asked for. He asked me what I wanted as I told him that Umut must have told him that. He nodded and told me that he needs one more month. I told him that in next 10 minutes his bank transfer would be done along with half of the advance for the next information. He said he would try to provide me as detailed information as he can access including bank accounts, shipping routes, weapons details etc.

Details of money trail routes and weapons smuggling along with assets recruitments for ISI was happening from Afghanistan, Iran and Syria. These assets were being moved into neighbouring countries of India. Umut was present in the meeting but was silent all throughout. Ruslan added that social media accounts of them did not exist, but they used gaming chats for communication a long and tested method. My time for the flight had come up as Umut offered to drop me back at home as Ruslan said to me that rest assured, I will get more information in the upcoming days.

I reached with Umut to the airport without any hassle, but I could not let my guard down as I knew that I still had a USB drive given by Ruslan containing the shipping routes and local funders name. I reached the Delhi office as I gave the drive to my desk chief. She was circumspect about the drive but after initial checks by our cyber team the drive was looked into. A password which Ruslan gave me was successful in getting us the location of possible attacks, shipping routes and the names of local organization working as money carriers. However, there was another subfolder named Code list. As soon as our desk chief clicked on that the drive got burnt. I decided to call Ruslan but could not get through. However, the real surprise came when I also could not reach Umut.

The cyber team of N.T.R.O. was sent in to check for the drive and my desk chief was informed at that precise moment that one of the local organizations mentioned there was indeed there in Punjab working as a community service centre for Sikhs. However, they have under suspicion list of the Punjab special forces intelligence unit. It was decided to go for a night raid and only one local police officer was informed based in the town just outside Ludhiana. When we entered the specific house all we found was a rotten body of someone shot dead at least three-four days earlier. Only a burnt piece of map was found which was collected by our forensic team and possibly were some local sensitive points where planning attacks took place or were funding collection meeting points.

The forensic team from only that fraction of map could identify the press from where it was printed. We called up their office and got information that their distributors sell detailed map of Indian cities. We asked for the local sellers list and after three days could identify two individuals who had bought the maps from Ludhiana. Our covert unit S.N.I.P.E.R. (Strategic National Intelligence Personnel for Evaluative Response) who were a specialized unit of N.I.A (National Investigation Agency) took into custody those two individuals. From them a handful of maps, pen drives and card of a Chinese company Chief Technical Officer specializing in cell phones were recovered.

Matching the fingerprints of the burnt map and the two unidentified assets taken into custody whose names were yet to be confirmed we could be sure that they were involved. Only thing we needed to confirm that a plan was being hatched but who was behind it. Those two had only confessed that a plan to disrupt Indian Space Program was on the agenda. The dotted lines may be referring to a larger attack through disruption of Indian assets via our space program.

The Mirror Behind The Mirror

The team that went in Punjab had recovered fingerprints and fragments of the map earlier as we did not get the postmortem report. Our cross verification from the two already in custody confirmed that he was the main carrier of money and weapons in the local areas of Punjab using a foundation as his cover. This spread over to Himachal, Haryana and Uttarakhand too. However right now we needed to focus on the Indian Space Program and points of possible cyber-attacks.

The Indian space program was looking at big ticket launches especially of the SAARC satellite and of the satellite destroying weapons system launch. Also at least two surveillance satellites were planned to be launched in the next 6 months. However, the USB drive that may have used to set an information trapping hook could also provide useful to us. The cyber team took around 6 hours of decryption and the trail of digital folders once saved on this drive from the internet bases in Istanbul were confirmed. Some of the folders which were deleted could be retrieved partially showed maps of Indian cities were downloaded and then deleted.

The S.N.I.P.E.R. team was keeping a watch on Kashmir especially on internet traffic generated from there and internet traffic being monitored from all possible sources of digital communication. The internet usage from cybercafes were easy to track but cell phones were difficult and so were other unconventional internet mediums.

I decided to go to Srinagar where a local contact had asked me to meet him. He told me that he wanted me to meet someone who was here in Kashmir. He was staying at a boat house and he wanted me to meet tonight at 9 p.m. I went at the location and boy there was a surprise for me. It was Umut and he was there with a bandage on his chin. He said that he had been double crossed by Ruslan and reached India four days before but did not reach him as he was being targeted by I.S.I. agents from Turkey.

Then he told me if I was looking to go after Ruslan it was useless as he himself was shot dead in his safehouse by I.S.I. (Inter Services Intelligence) agents. Umut said he came to know of it when he was in Dubai enroute to India. Ruksana and a very important ISI operative was involved in the operative. Also, a very close relative of Ruksana was posted in Delhi Embassy. There could be numerous plans to attack several installations, but he repeated that this time Indian Space based establishment would be the focus of the attack. However, I did not mention anything about the USB drive to Umut and the problems it caused to us.

We had installed recently the N.A.T.G.R.I.D. system and upgraded Israeli software. It was clear that the local ground planning was being directed through chat mechanism which was probably being done through gaming platform on in app mechanisms. However, as a precautionary mechanism we had put I.S.R.O. campus on high alert.

The entire cyber team was trying to snoop up information. But to no avail as even the cipher code and other investigative teams could not find anything substantive. The only strategy we could formulate was based on probably misleading information from either Umut or Ruslan. Still, we had to follow our leads and keep a watch on the port areas to investigate weapons and drugs coming in as well as increase security in strategic establishments including I.S.R.O. (Indian Space Research Organization), Airports etc.

Our team had been able to decrypt the USB drive further as some digital fragments of blueprints downloaded from someone's system about I.S.R.O. space programs were indeed found. Meanwhile the satellite launch was decided to take place very soon. However, to track Ruksana and her close associates the mother source of the USB drive and to which IP the files were being downloaded from in that drive was important to be accessed for preventing any further attack on ISRO or any other strategic establishment in India.

Although a week later there was an important breakthrough as an IP address was tracked to Turkey although it was hard to trace it. An onion web user through dark web using the name Blackbird was found to be the user. In the meantime, Umut called me as he had gone back to Turkey but had relocated to an unidentified location. He asked me to meet this time in Baku as he sent me his location.

He was staying at a safehouse as he asked me to meet around 8 p.m. and I reached at around 7:30 p.m. The safehouse was in an isolated location as Umut welcomed me and I asked him that whether he could provide me information on Jayesh who seemed to have disappeared from the radar and whether he could provide some insights. Umut said he would provide more information as he was going to get coffee for both of us. I kind of felt strange as he came back with the cup of coffee and as soon as I sipped the coffee, I could find that some more people had ventured into the room.

I asked Umut if I could finish my coffee as he nodded his head and then sipped his. As soon as he looked up, he stumbled and fell. The three were confused and before they could realize anything they too were neutralized. However how and why I had a backup team and how they were positioned on two sides of the windows has a different backstory which would come up later. The bodies were clean up by our sweeping team as Umut was only sedated and not dead as he was hit by a chemically laced bullet.

It was 6 hours later when Umut finally opened and said he was a part of the operation named Star Dot and his primary contact was Ruksana under the call sign black bird. He was her local contact in Turkey and helped her to move across locations like Azerbaijan, UAE and her local assets in the form of students recruited from India as well as Nepal, Pakistan, Sri-Lanka and Bangladesh. He said he had been specially asked by Ruksana to mislead our team so that she can work on her operation however they had to compromise Jayesh in the process.

Seeking The Truth Leads To A Bunch Of Lies

Time was running out as the space program was about to commence by the next week and that must go ahead by safeguarding it was our prime target. Umut started to divulge that the USB drive which he had given was to plant a source code for extracting information in whichever system the drive was inserted. Downloading system information in terms of the getting information on any kind of blueprint or information transcripts to be sold to the Chinese was the main motive.

Umut said that may be Ruksana was probably in Gaziantep in a safe house where she was waiting for the new trojan developed by Chinese and planted by the USB drive to provide real time information. We had to get to her as soon as possible as I called up the embassy and asked for an immediate flight arrangement to move to Gaziantep. They said they would call me back in half an hour. In the meantime, Umut named a safehouse located near a residential complex where she most likely could be as she was going to be in Turkey till the satellite launch as per the latest conversation, he had with her. After that she may out of Turkey for a while and take up a new deputation.

I received a call as our flight had been arranged from a private airport in Istanbul and it was a speculative move. Umut gave us the exact location of Ruksana's safehouse, but it was likely that there was only half a chance that she would be there. She may have either got information that Umut was untraceable and not being able to communicate on how his operation to take me out went ahead.

We went ahead and reached Gaziantep as in our flight we devised a plan to bring out Ruksana if she was in her safe house. The idea was to create commotion in the nearby residential complex as we got a rough blueprint of the location. In that commotion we had to take out Ruksana and get belongings from her place. A few litres of gasoline and Molotov cocktail was ready before hand as we reached the complex in the car of a local contact of Indian Embassy. Our team of 6 had already surrounded the building as we launched a few Molotov cocktails and chemical gas cannisters inside the complex. It was a $15^{\text{-floor}}$ complex, and all the people as planned had started to move out but there was nobody in the nearby one floor building as it was all dark. In the meantime, our team was looking out for Ruksana as we had entered the complex. One team went up to the building near the complex which was indeed empty. I was on the 6th floor as I investigated the room as the door seemed to be firmly shut and there were some noises coming from inside the room. As soon as I knocked on the door, I heard a male voice and in my broken Turkish asked them to evacuate. He told me to go away as it was at that precise moment I hit hard on the door as there were some other people who were coming down the stairs. They all banged on the door and asked them to come out when the door opened, and a flurry of bullets sprang across in the air with two people getting shot in the chest and the arm. In that commotion I took out my Glock from the back of my waist and fired at them as I entered the room and closed the door. Two of them were dead as the other one fired at me from behind the door which narrowly missed only for him to be shot point blank on his left eye.

Ruksana was standing against the wall close to her kitchen with a pouch in her hand which she was about to put up in flames. In the right time I managed to get hold of that as in the meantime the fire department and the police could be heard. A few more of the Molotov cocktails were thrown in all the balconies by our teams as planned.

The idea was to stall the fire brigade as we needed time to investigate the room. I managed to get into the other room and collected a few scraps of burnt paper. Also a few sticky notes containing names, dates and importantly two memory cards and an USB stick was found. The memory cards and the USB drive had sticky notes on each of them which had three different alphabets on them. Most likely they were indicative of what they contained.

The sticky notes recovered had the word Star Dots written on it in one of them. It needed to be seen if the sticky notes name and the ones on the memory card as well as the USB drive were cipher codes or not. However, we could not for much more time to decrypt those memory cards and USB drive. Meanwhile we needed to get out of Turkey as Ruksana was left unconscious by me before he could pull down my mask. We left for the airstrip as our flight by which we arrived would take us back to Ankara and from there to New Delhi. Meanwhile we had put our cyber team on work as the pictures of the memory card and the USB drive was sent to them apart from giving access to our laptop remotely.

Then the pandora's box opened as fortune seemed to be going our way as Ruksana was found to close to her safe house. Also, how we managed to get out of Ruksana's place with vital information in a country like Turkey was one part. Now the access to the satellite design, capabilities from satellite centre of Ahmedabad and I.S.R.O. in Bangalore were found in numerous folders with details. Also, several detailed information on communication satellites used for NATGRID were found. The team at Bangalore which was stationed and headed by Devendra Inamdar. I called up my desk chief Ranjini and told her that I would head to Bangalore to meet him to know the security details before the satellite launch went ahead. Ranjini gave a go ahead as she said she would also join me in due time.

Our cipher and cyber team had finally managed to crack the source code where the drive was first used. It was found to be a Pakistan Airforce base in Gilgit Baltistan area. Likely there was a trojan spyware in the drive which had been removed but was there before. Likely the drive was used in Pakistan and then brought into Turkey for further operations. The Prime Minister's office and national security advisor was informed by Ranjini my desk chief of the latest developments. However, a name called Srijan came up. The name was cross checked as the internet access based on that name was found in connection to Turkey and Indian Space Program used in codes which was decoded by our cipher and N.T.R.O. (National Technical Research Organization) cyber team. The name came up as the cyber team said information packets from Pakistan and China were downloaded in the office computer of someone in I.S.R.O. The local team on cross checking it found it to be belonging to a satellite design officer named Srijan Thakur.

The question was for how long the information was being downloaded and traded by him. I had managed to contact the local unit who said Srijan has been missing since yesterday afternoon and did not report for work today. Ranjini had also arrived in Bangalore as she said that her team had accessed information that likely they were traded to a certain asset in Pakistan who was sending it forward to China especially for the satellites and their observational capabilities in L.A.C. (Line of Actual Control).

A week later the plan for the S.A.A.R.C. satellite launch went ahead at around 11:30 p.m. from Sriharikota. There was a possible worry if this satellite information was completely compromised as some last-minute changes to its specification, operational capabilities and details were made to bypass the possible information compromise. However, after the launch of the satellite the hunt for Srijan was picking up. His last cell phone location was in Coimbatore. However, to find him would need a real miracle and that too in a very short span of time. The question of locating Srijan and how was he involved in all of this in connection with Ruksana and our whole operation rather than getting towards any closure had further complicated. Reports from multiple intelligence bureau and our special unit that got support from all of the intelligence agencies with a fancied acronym K.N.I.F.E.P.O.I. N.T. seemed to be failing. It was an agency that was meant to liaison information operating under Prime Minister's office with coordinating deputies from Home Minister, Ministry of External Affairs and Défense Ministry. It was meant to help and coordinate the different agencies for real time information gathering, sharing from NATGRID and taking covert action based on intelligence in coordination with R&AW (Research & Analysis Wing) and I.B. (Intelligence Bureau)

Operation Golden Crescent Triangle

The present mission codenamed "Operation Golden Crescent Triangle" became official much later but since the removal of 370, we were on this. Ground intelligence suggested that ISI had been pushing operatives around the country especially in Punjab and Northeast since Kashmir was getting out of bounds. However, there was also a coordinated attack map being planned with Naxals in the red corridor across India apart from the couriers and agents working for separatist groups of Khalistan and Northeast in Canada, U.K., USA, France and Germany etc. I was called back to Delhi where the idea was to form a coordinated response to the second independence movement threatening the integrity of India. I had already mailed my report from Istanbul a week back and things had got murkier since then. We were called here to determine how we had failed in locating a man that was our only link to the much-used word like national security! An entire coordinated team of expertise was at our disposal. My desk chief and PMO head was standing right next to me as the intelligence file reports from all the agencies were scattered right in front of me. PMO head Jagadeeshan seemed furious as he switched on the projector. It read "Operation Golden Crescent Triangle" as the slides moved ahead. The first slide had names of separatist Khalistan group members from Australia, Canada, France, Germany, U.K. and USA. In the second slide a flow chart of what was the plan of these separatist elements were planning. Three markers in the form of Naxals, Islamic radical groups and the separatist movements were highlighted with priority areas on the map of India. The ones who are reading this might want to know that why was this named "Operation Golden Crescent Triangle" became evident later.

However first we had to locate our missing scientist and finally our technological apparatus looked to come into effect. Ramesh Prasad a postmaster at Raipur, Rupesh Bagchi a professor from Delhi were our two links operating as covert agents to provide inputs on the urban supply lines towards deeper red corridor operators. They have failed on many occasions but were important pivotal points on many occasions. We had two more important assets under our deep covert security plan. For the last 10 years, Laxmi Devi a Dalit and a widow from Samastipur, Bihar and Rupa a young local from Sambalpur for the last two years had been operating specifically on the red corridor intelligence program. They were a part of the dangerous program where they had to carry on their local lives and also mingle with elements on ground to provide local human intel support to us. They had been providing local support in terms of gathering data on the new leaders, possible coordination with ISI leaders as well as other separatist elements. The latest reports suggested that there were some truck movements happening at Raxaul for the last 10 days and it may have connection with our missing space scientist and some nefarious plans. Although that would come up in the next part of the story. For this part of the story, it was about finding the missing space scientist Srijan.

However still we did not about how we will wrap up the case of missing SAARC satellite and the missing ISRO scientist. So, before I lose you guys on so many things there are two parts of the story. In this part the first part on the missing S.A.A.R.C. (South Asian Association for Regional Cooperation) satellite and ISRO scientist. Let us go back to the covert agents who have been tailing other persons of interest with reasonable Maoists interests. However, there was a lot of questions left unanswered from our covert "Operation Cobalt" carried out at Istanbul. From that strike carried out, we recovered an USB drive. The USB stick did help us to find out a few important map's location, blueprints of satellite had a few more pictures and documents pointing towards a more sinister future. National Investigation Agency, Intelligence Bureau, Research and Analysis Wing had been tasked by Prime Minister's Office to set up a coordinated response with our liaison agency. Everyone wanted to know where was the location of the missing I.S.R.O. scientist? NSA (National Security Agency) chief advisor called me and my desk chief alone to his room and asked me what I thought based on my first-hand encounter with Ruksana. Also, he pushed up the second question that was there any other kinds of information that I had access to that could possibly tell us more about this missing S.A.A.R.C. satellite. I said that the story would not end with this satellite saga and there was more at play. We had not been able to pinpoint anything directly to Ruksana anyways and we could not take it up with Pakistan or any other multilateral forums before getting solid evidence. However, for the current conundrum, time was precious to us. The USB drive was protected by biometric as it was important for us to get the details of the map marking and possible person of interest list. It took about 3 hours to crack the USB drive biometric firewall getting help from a private contractor named Pink Swan. There was always a risk to get private contractors involved but we were desperate and as they say desperate times needs desperate measures. The USB drive got us maps of Srilanka navy port at Colombo. There was a separate folder with the name of the scientist marked in it. Along with his name there was a cipher code which after decryption got us coordinates near Guntur, Andhra Pradesh. This seemed to coordinate with our local covert operatives whom I mentioned earlier sending us reported that the Andhra Pradesh Maoist groups were being reactivated with weapons being pushed from north through Chhattisgarh. We received a call from Guntur local police station which was closest to the coordinates that a missing file had been registered from the missing person's mother. However, after three days she too had been missing. Related to that incident, search was on and finally on receiving a national lookout notice, Kerala police had found two unidentified bodies near a Cochin village. Both had bullet marks which had been found after postmortem from a gun made in Gaziantep, Turkey. Interestingly there have been suicide notes found alongside both the bodies "I died and killed my only family member because of the shame I had brought forth to my country". The gun although found in Turkey was accessible in India and had even been used in certain areas in Uttar Pradesh, Maharashtra in recent times. The body had been taken charge from the local police by our southern deputation office Krishna Aiyanagar. I was asked to immediately report to Cochin and taken jurisdiction of the matter as our special unit had special powers under National Security Act apart from National Investigation Agency. After hopping on a flight which took 3 hours for me to reach from one part of the country Delhi to another part Cochin.

The NIA local officer was already on spot and was waiting for me to pick me up from the Airport to take me the police morgue where the bodies were kept. He said that some of the local villagers saw the dead bodies floating on the local lake from where it was fished out. A local diary was found with the body of the man which had most of the pages washed away except for a few entries that could be retrieved to be about his early childhood. The local NIA officer continued speaking about him mentioned that he was indeed a super talented man with top of the class at IISC Bangalore, satellite engineering program and then at USA for his doctorate. It was during that program that he got embroiled with some wrong elements and the name Ruksana popped up. He had mentioned that he used to like her but after being 14 years apart they only reconnected three years back as they met at a conference in Stockholm, Sweden on space security. He went there as a rookie satellite engineer and Ruksana as a young diplomat just got posted there. India was working on a new cooperative project on a space program. He went there for a project, but he had known Ruksana long before since his days in USA. During their time at Cornell University in USA he and Ruksana came in contact. They quickly developed a bond which developed into an intimate romantic relationship. He finished his Ph.D. program and moved to Texas for Texas instruments. They did keep in touch as Ruksana finished her master's and was in Washington D.C. where he got a position as a local liaison officer for Pakistan Embassy. They were apart by miles but kept in touch. It was one fine morning around 2016 that he got a call from Ministry of Telecommunications for a project which needed satellite engineer for a project with Ericsson in Stockholm. Surprisingly at that same time there was a meeting of the international donors where Pakistan had sent a team of two and amongst them was Ruksana. It was around the time of the summer and on 20th June they meet in Stockholm at a café. Although they had to split up when he moved to India, however they have kept in touch through communication. Then Sweden happened and on that evening they finally met. The reading continued from the notes which were from a small notebook. "We had long island iced tea as we caught up over a lot of things. Ruksana told me that she had joined Pakistan diplomatic circles and was getting her feet in the political circles. I told her that I was working on the Indian Space program especially the satellite division. She seemed elated. That night was romantic as we decided to give our relationship a try and decided to travel at regular intervals. We both decided to keep our relationship a secret from our respective governments. What started as our relationship for over a year which my family were oblivious to as well took a turn for something sinister a year and half later. I found it a day when I received a mail with all the pictures of me in an intimate position and the mail read either all of this gets leaked, or you agree to what we want you to do. Love Ruksana. Well, when I read this, the very first thing I felt about myself was I am an idiot and had been used even if cliched as it sounds. My heart was racing that whether I need to end my life then or do I need to fall further in the pit. The latter happened.

Falling further in the pit with strings attached

"I was asked to send copies of the blueprints of the upcoming SAARC satellite project. I had never mentioned to it before but well I did say certain other things amongst which there was a conversation about this collaborative project. I just had told her that Pakistan was the only country being omitted from this project and in a matter of around 18-20 months it would be launched. Then as fate would have had it all of this happened. I started to sulk at my office and even if I started to feel suicidal, I kept continuing. However, I was sending out information on the satellite project coming up and also feeding intel on two our geo stationary satellite that had been positioned for monitoring the India-Pakistan-Afghanistan border area that also had oversight on Iran to Central Asia till Turkey's eastern region. I was still a junior assistant and did not have clearance to get access to satellite movements at precise times. However, I did manage to get my hands on the coordinates. I always wondered that what was she going to do with all these information". The reading stopped as there was no entry until after that it read in half a page "I knew that since I had given access to the ISI till this week as the SAARC satellite is up there, I feel I have ultimately betrayed my country but the coordinate information that would be received constantly by the bug placed in the satellite has put my country at risk. However, I have also placed a jammer that would take into account transmitting signal to be tracked by anyone who are not a part of the core group. That is the satellite would autolock feeding its signal to anyone outside the core scientist group and their secured access system to get access to real time updates from the satellite. So finally, the launch has taken place and I know I am running out of time as Ruksana would try to squeeze out more work from me." Then the writing stopped again until the very day of his death. "I did not see this coming and before I have decided, my life is in danger. If I am found dead, I want my people to forgive me". The diary ended there as the forensic part of me told my heart that he had thrown the bag before the shootout happened. Three shots, two from Rakesh and one shot from the other. Then we happened to be here but a lot of things to dial back upon.

Dialling back upon the Ratcliffe Line

The postmortem reports were due in another 15 hours, however the other body seemed to be of Ruksana which seemed quite an embarrassment for us. That is how a high-profile Pakistani target after whom we were targeting had managed to break into our nation and that too getting hold of the national secrets. However, the only positive thing is that if it was indeed Ruksana, we could get hold of lot of information although it meant a lot of diplomatic crises as well with Pakistan. Most importantly, how did she manage to enter our territory and what was she really remained a mystery. The postmortem reports came in after 15 hours as the bodies was kept in the mortuary till then. The reports confirmed that indeed the other body was of Ruksana. She had entered on a forged Canadian passport via Bangalore. She was carrying no luggage, but she was found in a car that had a registration number which did not match any records as it was quite natural. However, the make of the car and the national highway was identified as three people other than Ruksana were seen deboarding from the car. The car was found to be abandoned near the Andhra Pradesh-Odisha border but then her movements till Guntur was unresolved. Also, not to forget that what was she doing here with those three mysterious people also needed to be found out. Ultimately those were the answers as to where the damage that Srijan had done even if unwillingly and what could be the aftereffect of all this. The postmortem had however something interesting as the reports mentioned she was found to be using contacts which were not just ordinary lenses but was a synthetic cornea-based lens that could capture images. For me it seemed like a fiction movie stuff however this helped us later. Although to get hold of those lens from IB, Police Department as well as R&AW was another departmental battle but being a special unit under Défense and Home Ministry we got preference. The next part of the story would follow.

www.ingramcontent.com/pod-product-compliance
Lightning Source LLC
LaVergne TN
LVHW041643070526
838199LV00053B/3526